The Airs of Tillie

Books by Barbara Casey

Fiction
The Airs of Tillie
Slightest in the House
Just Like Family
The House of Kane
The Coach's Wife
The Gospel According to Prissy

Young Adult Fiction
The F.I.G. Mysteries
The Cadence of Gypsies
The Wish Rider
The Clock Flower
The Nightjar's Promise
The Seraphim's Song

Nonfiction
Kathryn Kelly: The Moll behind Machine Gun Kelly
Assata Shakur: A 20th Century Escaped Slave
Velvalee Dickinson: The Doll Woman Spy

Coming Soon!
Shyla's Initiative

The Airs of Tillie

Barbara Casey

SPEAKING VOLUMES, LLC
NAPLES, FLORIDA
2023

The Airs of Tillie

Copyright © 2023 by Barbara Casey

ISBN 978-1-64540-975-5

For my mother, whose love and support, and her pure joy of life, is a constant source of inspiration.

Prologue

The spectators in the stands applauded politely as the beautiful Arabian horse named Arabesque was coaxed onto the stadium field by its young rider, Tillie Turpning.

"That girl won't even make it over the first jump," a man whispered to his wife.

"Why do you say that?" The woman studied the small figure sitting astride the large black animal.

"She's never ridden in competition before," he answered. "And look at her. She's so small compared to the other riders in her age group. There's no way she can handle a horse the size of Arabesque, and especially one as temperamental." The woman nodded and fanned her face briskly with the program she had been given. August was always hot in south Florida, and it had been especially so this year. There had even been talk about canceling the Equestrian Gold Cup, but in the end it was decided the prestigious event would take place as scheduled.

A gentle breeze stirred, scattering red and white petals from the potted geraniums that were decorating the field. The crowd noises softened. Arabesque picked up her gate into a slow gallop around the outer edge of the jumping arena in response to Tillie's silent command, settling into her own pace, her natural rhythm. Then she felt the pressure of the young girl's knees on her sides—another command, another signal from rider to horse. Arabesque began galloping faster, her eyes alert and focused on a split-rail fence banked with hedges. Faster, faster, up, and over, and Arabesque once again resumed her slow gallop.

This time she felt the reins pull slightly to the left. She angled her strong, muscular body in that direction and once again picked up speed. Three stone walls, each positioned in front of the other, blocked her path. "You can do it," she heard the girl whisper. As Arabesque approached the first wall at a full gallop, she felt the girl shift her weight, working with her own, blending her body movement with that of the horse. Over the first wall, the second, and then the third. Arabesque snorted loudly and bobbed her head with exuberance. But she wasn't finished yet. Again the girl pressed her knees, silently instructing and urging Arabesque to perform.

They negotiated three more jumps: the oxer, the tiger trap, and the vertical gate. So far their score was perfect. The crowd was totally quiet now as they watched the champion jumper obey the commands of its young rider.

The water hazard was next. Tillie and Arabesque had watched three other horses lose points on it, and one horse had to be disqualified for refusing to jump it at all. "You're not afraid, Arabesque," the horse heard Tillie whisper. Faster, faster the horse galloped toward the hazard. Up she went, once again feeling the young girl's tensed body stretched in union with her own. They were over it. Arabesque looked across the field and saw Molly, her companion horse, watching.

"Good girl, Arabesque. Good girl." But Tillie wouldn't let Arabesque relax. The horse felt pressure, this time coming from the girl's heels and knees. Arabesque continued in her rhythm. Two more jumps to go, and they were also the most difficult. Arabesque felt the girl urge her to pick up her gate. She didn't understand that they had only a limited amount of time to complete the jumps or otherwise lose points. She only sensed she had to hurry; and that if she didn't, for some reason the girl would be disappointed.

Arabesque felt the girl press her knees harder into her sides and turned toward the obstruction. Bales of hay were stacked into a five-foot barrier. Extending from both ends were fence rails of varying lengths. Arabesque perked her ears forward, her breathing was heavier now. Closer and closer she galloped toward the obstruction until she felt the girl's body tense. Through the air they went, and when they landed on the other side, the barrier was still intact.

Murmurings could be heard from the crowd. So far, this young girl who had never ridden in competition before had scored higher than any of the other contestants in the Youth Division. There was one jump left—the dreaded spiderwort—and only fifteen seconds remaining on the clock.

Arabesque circled to the right obeying the pull of the reins and then faced the spiderwort head on. "Just one more, Arabesque. You can do it."

Once again Arabesque felt the girl's heels and knees pressing into her body. The horse immediately responded, stretching into a full gallop toward the obstacle. The dirt beneath her hooves was loose and unstable, dug up by the other horses who had jumped before her. Because of the angles and different sizes of the railings, Arabesque lost her sense of perspective. She couldn't judge the distance of when to make her jump. But the girl had a tight hold on the reins. She would know. And Arabesque trusted the girl.

Suddenly Arabesque felt Tillie tense her body and lean forward. When she did, Arabesque jumped with all the strength she had left. And when she landed, she galloped as hard as she could to the finish line.

The crowd erupted into cheers and applause. Arabesque felt the young girl's arms around her neck, hugging her, stroking her. "You did it, Arabesque, you did it! Good girl," she said over and over again. "Good girl."

JUNE

Chapter One

Matt waited in the darkness of his room until he no longer heard his parents stirring around. Quietly he slipped down the stairs and out the back door. He didn't like sneaking around, but if his parents knew, they would be upset. His dad especially. Even though they didn't attend church much, they had been brought up as Baptists—Southern Baptists. His dad barely tolerated other Christian religions, so he definitely wouldn't understand why his son was going to the mosque for prayer meetings. No, it was better they not know—not yet, anyway.

Matt jogged down the road to where he was supposed to meet his friend, Mustafa. As usual, Mustafa was already there waiting. Matt climbed into the shiny black truck, grateful for the ride, and grinned at his friend.

"So, you escape again, huh?"

Matt nodded even though it bothered him that Mustafa thought that he had to "escape" from his parents. He would have to tell them soon. After all, he was almost eighteen—a man. He could make his own decisions about what religion he chose to follow.

Mustafa broke into Matt's thoughts. "Abdullah is coming tonight. This is a great honor for our group. He is an important leader. You will meet him."

Matt had heard a lot about Abdullah not only from Mustafa but from others who attended the prayer meetings. He had even overheard some of them talking about Abdullah being Al Queda. That bothered Matt. After all, it was the Al Queda who had flown those planes into the twin towers in New York and the Pentagon. Another plane had crashed in that field in Pennsylvania. All because of the Al Queda terrorists. He had asked Mustafa about it, but Mustafa only told him that Muslims were against terrorism but that jihad was among a Muslim's divine legal rights to be used to defend himself and his people and to spread Islam. Matt wasn't sure he understood, but he didn't want to push it. After all, he was the one who had asked to be invited to the mosque. For now, he would just learn as much as he could about Islam by attending the prayer meetings and reading the Qur'an, a book Mustafa had given him. Then he would decide if it was the religion for him. So far, everything he had learned was good.

Mustafa parked the truck in front of his father's small grocery store. Across the street a group of young Muslim men had already congregated in front of the mosque. Matt recognized most of them from previous meetings. All of them seemed glad to see him and spoke. It made him feel important. Not like at home where the only thing that mattered was taking care of Mabe's needs. No one cared whether he needed anything or not. Just so long as he worked and got paid. He couldn't even keep all of the money he earned—he had to give most of it to his mom to help with the bills. Here at least he was accepted as a man. They liked him. And the few times he had been asked to express his opinion, they had liked what he had to say. "You are like a brother," Mustafa had told him. "You are one of us."

Matt sat next to Mustafa and glanced around the room. The boy sitting in front of him—probably no more than twelve—turned around and smiled. Matt was glad he had come, even if it did mean sneaking out of the house.

* * *

The soft pastels of yellow, pink, and magenta gently pushed upwards on the horizon. It would be daylight soon. Motionless, Tillie watched through the unshuttered window above her bed. In the distance she could just make out the darkened shape of a large, sprawling, two-story house and its steep-pitched roof. Beyond the house she could see another large structure, and beside it something long and built closer to the ground. It was the barn and stables. Tillie sighed and shifted her weight ever so slightly so as not to disturb her sister sleeping in the bed next to her. She pushed her face closer to the open window and breathed deeply. They had been clearing the cane fields for several weeks now, and the air was filled with the sweet, pungent scent of burnt raw sugar.

Tillie had been awake for what seemed like hours, listening to the night sounds, watching, and waiting. Maybe this was the wrong day. But it had always been the first Thursday in June, she argued with herself. Just then a flicker of light caught her attention, and she saw a car slowly move away from the big house. It turned from the driveway onto the blacktop road that ran between the cane fields and the pastures. Tillie could feel the excitement rising inside her. She had been right after all. It was today. Today the big girl would come home.

Tillie watched the car stop at the end of the blacktop road and then turn east onto the main highway toward Palm Beach. When she could no longer see its taillights, she quietly slipped off her bed. Tillie hadn't pulled the covers down the night before so she wouldn't have to waste time making her bed. Besides, it had been a warm night and very little breeze. It would have been too hot with covers. Mabe, her sister, had thought Tillie was playing a game, but she wouldn't sleep on top of her covers. She always slept under a faded blue spread. It didn't matter to Mabe how hot it was.

Tillie looked over at Mabe to make sure she was still asleep. She didn't want to wake her before she normally got up or she would be cross. On the foot of Mabe's bed was a ratty looking purple and green Easter basket. Its handle was positioned exactly perpendicular to the horizontal floorboards because that was the only way Mabe would go to sleep. In it was a pad of drawing paper, some charcoal pencils, and an assortment of broken crayons and colored chalk. Cardboard had been taped over the bottom and around the sides of the basket so nothing could fall out.

During the day Mabe took it, along with her spread, wherever she went. Sitting on her spread she would draw the things around her as she saw them. It was as though the spread defined the physical boundaries of her world, and drawing was her way of communicating from that world.

The doctor said Mabe was autistic. Tillie didn't understand exactly what that meant. She just knew that she loved her pretty older sister, and that Mabe was special. Mabe did and saw things in a way no one else could, like the way she talked in a secret language, and the way she could draw usual, every-day objects and make them look unusual. Tillie looked around the room, her eyes pausing briefly on each of the many sheets of paper that had been thumb-tacked to the walls. Colorful blobs of crayon and chalk; irregular lines drawn with charcoal and pencil. Tillie thought they were beautiful.

Tillie glanced once more at the expressionless face of her sleeping sister as she quickly brushed the wrinkles from her bed. Then she pulled on her faded red shorts, her old, dirty sneakers, and a cast-off tee-shirt that had once belonged to her big brother Matt. She liked wearing Matt's old shirts, even if he was six years older and eighty pounds heavier. By the time he finished with them, they were just getting nice and soft. The sleeves were usually torn, but Tillie didn't mind. She just ripped the sleeves off anyway, or if they were torn just a little, she would roll them up in neat, tight folds.

Next to Tillie's bed on a three-legged oak stool was a stack of clean, neatly folded hankies and a worn, somewhat cumbersome-looking book entitled MISS ANNE'S BOOK OF ETIQUETTE AND OTHER IMPORTANT THINGS. Tillie picked out a clean hanky from the pile and stuffed it into her side pocket. "Miss Anne says a lady should always have a clean hanky with her," she whispered to herself, unconcerned that the cherished book she quoted from had been printed in another century and another place. Picking up the heavy book, she sat down on the floor next to Mabe's bed and began to read silently to herself in the early-morning light coming through the window: *It is polite for a young person to offer his or her seat to an older person.*

"Doke," murmured Mabe. It was exactly 7:15. Mabe always woke up at 7:15. And, like always, Tillie's mom had picked out the night before what clothes Mabe was to wear. So all Tillie had to do was to make sure her sister got them on right. This wasn't easy since Mabe didn't like to be touched. But she seemed to tolerate Tillie better than anyone else in the family, so it was Tillie who always helped her. Besides, at eleven years of age, Tillie was also the youngest so she had more time in the mornings than the rest of her family. Especially now that she was out of school for summer break.

Mabe went to a special school every morning for half a day, even during the summer, because the doctor said it was important for her to be exposed to external experiences and stay in a fixed routine. Sometimes Tillie and her parents went to Mabe's school too, but just to visit. Matt didn't go. Tillie couldn't tell if Mabe liked school and being exposed to external experiences or not. But as long as she could take her spread and basket with her, she didn't usually make a fuss. And she was learning things, like how to clap her hands in rhythm to music and how to feed herself using a fork and spoon.

"Doke," Mabe repeated getting out of bed. Sometimes Mabe talked in regular sentences. Other times she would go for days without saying anything. Then there were those times when she would only say one word, like "doke." No one understood what she meant by it, but Tillie thought it was part of the secret language that Mabe knew and that it meant *Tillie*.

Tillie led Mabe into the small bathroom that adjoined their bedroom and gave her a wet washcloth so she could wash her face. Then she put toothpaste on Mabe's toothbrush so she could brush her teeth. Tillie always did everything for Mabe the same way and in the same order. That way Mabe wouldn't get upset. When they had finished in the bathroom, the two girls went back to the bedroom where Tillie began handing Mabe her clothes to put on. Mabe used to not be able to dress herself, but that was one of the things she learned in school.

So far, so good. Tillie hoped Mabe wouldn't be difficult this morning. Sometimes if she got real upset she would miss her ride to school, and then Tillie would have to help her mom take care of her at home. But today Tillie had something important to do, and she wanted to make sure Mabe didn't miss her ride.

"Today's the first Thursday in June," Tillie said handing Mabe a clean sock to put on. "The big girl gets home today."

"Doke, Thursday," Mabe answered.

"That's right." Tillie smiled.

When Mabe was finally dressed, Tillie gently brushed her soft blond hair. That was the only time Mabe liked for Tillie to touch her. Then Tillie fastened a barrette in Mabe's hair to keep it out of her eyes. It was so fine and silky. Her dad said it was like angel hair.

"Oh oh," said Mabe, her face starting to get red. And then a little louder as she slapped the side of her head and repeated, "Oh oh."

Tillie immediately removed the barrette. "Please, Mabe, don't make a fuss. Not this morning."

Tillie watched Mabe's face once again become vague and expressionless. Her breathing became regular. She was all right. Her anger had passed. Tillie hurriedly made up Mabe's bed and handed her the folded spread and basket. Then she picked up the heavy book she had been reading earlier. Clutching it against her chest, she carefully led Mabe down the narrow wooden stairs.

* * *

"Don't let it drop! Don't let it drop!" Melissa Markham squealed from her bunk bed while she stomped her feet on the bare hardwood floor.

"That's mighty easy for you to say," Jewel panted to her roommate as she scrambled to bounce the slightly deflated soccer ball off her head. Ellen and Sue, who also shared the dormitory room, lunged toward the gray flying sphere only to find themselves moments later sprawled on the floor laughing. It was the kind of uncontrolled laughter that comes not because the situation was all that funny, but because the four girls had gotten very little sleep the night before—their last night at Sweet Palms Boarding School before the start of summer vacation. And they all had a very bad case of the silly giggles.

Bouncing the soccer ball from their heads had been a favorite tension-reliever of the four roommates during their sophomore year together at Sweet Palms. Now that exams were finally over and the girls were all going their separate ways for the summer, it seemed only appropriate that Jewel, Ellen, Sue, and Melissa participate one last time in this silly, idiotic pastime.

As usual, Melissa had tired first—perhaps because she was quite a bit heavier than the other three. Or maybe because, even in spite of the close relationship she had with her roommates, she still felt somewhat inhibited and self-conscious around them. It was funny to watch her friends act ridiculous, but Melissa couldn't quite let herself be that spontaneous. Bouncing a soccer ball on her head made her body do awkward things and pose in strange, unnatural positions. And Melissa didn't want to draw any more attention to her overweight body than she had to.

Sue thrust her arm under Melissa's bed for the ball. When she pulled her hand out, along with the ball was a clump of dust and an unopened bag of fun-size Snicker candy bars. Melissa's heart thudded in her ears, and she could feel beads of sweat begin to form on her upper lip. All semester she had bragged to her friends about how she was losing weight by eating mostly pineapple. She had been so careful to pick out only the pineapple dishes at mealtimes as further proof to her friends that she was indeed maintaining a diet and losing weight. Sue's discovery of the hidden bag of Snickers, however, destroyed in one instant all of that deception.

Sue, not only the most aggressive of the four girls but the most outspoken one as well, immediately saw through Melissa's so-called "pineapple diet" and burst into a succession of snorts, hiccups, and giggles. The truth is, each of Melissa's roommates had suspected she was sneaking food. After all, when four girls live in an area the size of a turkey platter, it is rather hard to disguise the sound of food packages being opened and food being chewed—even if it is done under a pillow in the middle of the night. And, also, there was the simple fact that Melissa didn't look like she was losing weight. But they hadn't wanted to embarrass Melissa by confronting her with their suspicions; that is, until now. Suddenly, on this first Thursday in June and the end of their sophomore year in high school, it didn't seem to matter anymore—at least not to Sue.

"So, Melissa, been holding out, have we?" she said in her most mocking voice, puffing out her cheeks and patting her pooched stomach. She flicked the dust ball from her hand and snorted. "Stuffing ourselves with a little extra something to go along with all those pineapple chunks?"

Ellen giggled nervously. Jewel, who was not only Melissa's roommate but her best friend as well, watched Melissa's face turn into a red glow with embarrassment.

"Those Snickers are mine," Jewel snapped. "I was going to surprise ya'all with them as a going-away present before we have to leave this morning," she continued rapidly, "but leave it to you, Sue, to go snooping around where you don't belong."

Sue stopped snorting and giggling long enough to glance from Melissa to Jewel. "Well, I don't care who they belong to as long as I get some," she said somewhat miffed.

Jewel snatched the bag of candy dangling from Sue's hand and tore it open. Then she divided the sixteen small bars into four piles on the bed next to where Melissa was sitting and passed them out. "Happy summer vacation," she said, sounding cheerful once again. Her eyes lingered only a slight moment on Melissa's face when she handed her the four small bars of candy. Melissa looked at Jewel with relief and gratitude and then down at the candy in her hands.

Sue, Jewel, and Ellen quickly ripped the wrappings from the candy and stuffed it into their mouths.

"I'll just save mine," Melissa said quietly.

Sue snorted and started to say something, but Jewel quickly grabbed up the soccer ball and threw it at her. The head-butting game was once again under way.

"Jewel, Sue, Ellen!" yelled a tall, thin girl with equally tall, thin hair from the door of their dorm room. "Your parents are waiting downstairs."

Stick, as the four roommates had nicknamed the yelling girl, had been hall monitor for the term, and it had been a constant source of annoyance to them at how much she relished the little bit of authority that title gave her.

"O.K., grits," the girl barked impatiently. "So get your carcasses out of here." Then looking at Melissa, she sang in a false note of sweetness, "Your daddy sent the car again for you."

For the second time in just a few minutes, Melissa felt the uncomfortable sweat of embarrassment. This time Sue didn't snort and giggle, though. In fact, no one said anything. Instead, everyone seemed to find something fascinating to stare at in the vicinity of the floor. Not once had Melissa's father been to see her during the school year. When all the other parents came for Open House, her dad had been too busy to come. So Jewel had invited her to go to the picnic and the soccer game and all the other planned campus activities with her family, which included in addition to Jewel and her parents, four brothers and two sisters. Even though they tried to make her feel like she was just another one of "The Tribe," as they called themselves, Melissa couldn't help feeling like she was intruding. More than that, she resented that her father hadn't come to the Open House after saying that he would.

At Thanksgiving, Melissa had made her dad promise he wouldn't send the car, but he would come pick her up himself to take her home for the holidays. After all, it was only an hour's drive from Markham Farms. He could surely spare that much time. And he would be able to meet her roommates. But when the time came, he had sent the car for Melissa. The same thing happened for the Christmas and spring holidays. So when Stick bellowed out about her father sending the car again, Melissa felt hurt and angry and embarrassed, but not really surprised.

"Move it," Stick yelled once more.

Everyone stopped staring at the floor and began hurriedly gathering up an assortment of duffel bags, shoulder bags, suitcases, and paper sacks in a flurry of last-minute hugs. Jewel waited behind with Melissa and watched Ellen and Sue noisily bound out the door and down the hall, dragging and bumping their bags along with them and yelling their good-byes.

When the others had left, Melissa put her fleshy arms around Jewel and hugged her. "I'm really going to miss you. Remember what you promised. You are going to write to me."

"I'm going to miss you, too. And speaking of writing…" Jewel reached into one of her sacks—the one stuffed with dirty clothes—and pulled out an envelope. "I have already written to you, but you can't read it until you get home."

Melissa laughed and took the envelope. "I guess this means that I already owe you a letter."

Jewel gathered the last of her bags together. "Don't let those horses throw you," she said smiling.

After Jewel disappeared down the hall, Melissa sat back down on her bed and looked around the quiet, deserted room. The envelope Jewel had given her wasn't sealed. She opened it and pulled out the single sheet of notebook paper. *"Don't forget to write! Love ya, Jewel."* Melissa stuck the paper back into the envelope and pushed it into the front pocket of her jeans. Then she picked up the four bars of candy and carefully opened each one, pulling the wrappers apart at the ends so as not to rip the paper unevenly. Slowly she began eating them. When she finished, she crushed the wrappers and threw them into the trash can. Then she grabbed her bags and jerked up her suitcase and walked out the door.

* * *

Molly stuck her head out of the opening of her barn stall, stomped her foot impatiently, and snorted loudly. She couldn't understand why she hadn't been allowed to go to the north pasture with Arabesque and the other horses. She was always allowed to be with Arabesque. She and Arabesque were best friends. Molly could find the best patches of green clover, and Arabesque, with her long beautiful black tail, knew just how to stand so it would brush the flies and other insects from Molly's face.

Molly shook her mane and whinnied irritably. She sniffed the air. She sensed that the man who smelled like leather, tobacco, and wild cherries was approaching. Pushing against the stall door she perked her ears forward and leaned farther out of the opening.

"Hello, Molly, old girl." The man approached easily, lifted the latch on the door to the stall and entered. "How are you feeling today?" he asked, patting the horse's neck and gently stroking her sides and stomach. "Feels like your milk has come in," he said as he expertly massaged Molly's teats. "Got some waxing there." He wiped the moisture from his hand onto his trousers and continued talking soothingly to Molly as he stroked and examined her. "Guess we'd better get Doc out here this morning. It won't be long now." He patted Molly once more on the neck and left, pulling the stall door closed behind him.

Molly didn't understand what the man who smelled like leather, tobacco and wild cherries said. She only knew that she missed her best friend, Arabesque, very much and wanted to be with her. Molly neighed crossly and pushed against her stall door. Much to her surprise, it opened. She took a couple of steps forward and looked in the direction of where the man had gone. When she didn't see him, she walked through the corral and out the gate leading toward the north pasture. She felt tired and heavy, but some sweet clover would make her feel better—some sweet clover and being with her best friend, Arabesque.

When she got to the open pasture, she took several deep breaths trying to smell Arabesque and the other horses. But there was smoke in the air, and she couldn't pick up their scent. Ears perked forward, she began to trot. She had no sooner taken a few steps, however, when she felt a sharp stabbing pain in her side. She stopped for a moment, breathing deeply and trying to relax. Then she started walking again in a northerly direction to where the pasture met the sugarcane field. That was where the best clover grew.

Molly went only a few more yards when she felt another sharp pain, this one stretching across her stomach. Suddenly she felt frightened. She looked back toward the stables, but she knew she wouldn't be able to walk that far. A short distance ahead was a small grove of trees. If she could just get to some shade and rest a little, she would be all right. She walked sluggishly toward the trees, feeling pain with each step she took. When she finally reached the trees, she lay down in the nearest grassy area. If only Arabesque were there. She would swish her beautiful long black tail to keep the flies and other insects away. Molly whinnied softly as the pain grew worse. Then she lay her head down on the soft green grass.

Chapter Two

"Well, there are my early birds!" Evelyn Turpning smiled at her two daughters. She was standing in front of the stove stirring a large blue enamel pot of oatmeal. With the weather being much too hot for the every-day jeans she usually wore, she had put on a loose-fitting summer dress that buttoned up the front, and her straight, gray hair was tied up off her neck with a yellow ribbon. The windows and the back door were open, and a small fan sitting on one end of the counter was noisily circulating hot air from one side of the room to the other.

Tillie poured herself and Mabe a glass of orange juice and sat down opposite the fan. Carefully she placed a paper napkin across Mabe's lap and then her own, just the way it said to do in MISS ANNE'S BOOK OF ETIQUETTE AND OTHER IMPORTANT THINGS.

"The big girl gets home today," Tillie said, sipping her juice.

"Now, Tillie," said her mother, looking up from her stirring, "that's none of your business. You have enough to do around here today without worrying about Capt'n Mark's daughter getting home. And her name is Melissa."

Tillie's mom put an apple that had been sliced into wedges and a piece of plain toast on a plate and set it in front of Mabe. Then she thwacked a clump of oatmeal with a wooden spoon into a large ceramic bowl and handed it to Tillie. "Not too much sugar," she said watching Tillie reach for the bowl filled with brown granules. That was one advantage to having a father who was cut foreman of the Markham Farms. They could get all the raw sugar crystals they wanted for nothing. Tillie waited until her mom turned back to the stove and then put three heaping scoops of sugar into her bowl.

The screen door suddenly swung open and Tillie's dad and brother, Matt, clomped into the kitchen wearing their heavy boots and aluminum shields that covered their legs and hands. They had already been out to the barracks where most of the field workers stayed and checked on who wouldn't be able to work in the cane that day.

Glancing at Mabe, Matt grumbled, "Are you still here?" Mabe either didn't hear him or she simply chose to ignore him, focusing instead on poking her finger into a slice of toast. Matt removed the shields from his hands and then spooned some sugar into his mug of coffee. He was always in a bad mood early in the morning, especially when he had been out late the night before. Tillie knew he had been sneaking out at night after everyone else was in bed and it worried her. But she wouldn't say anything.

Tillie would have liked to tell him that Capt'n Mark's daughter was coming home today. And if she watched from her special hiding place in the wild virgin cane and Napier grass that grew alongside the road by the big house, she would be able to see what the girl wore and how she fixed her hair. Matt wouldn't understand, or course. He would only laugh at her for putting on "airs" as he called it. Like when she kept checking out MISS ANNE'S BOOK OF ETIQUETTE AND OTHER IMPORTANT THINGS from the library. She checked it out so often that Mrs. Lyles, the librarian, finally gave it to Tillie. The book was out of print anyway and much too old-fashioned for what most of the library patrons wanted to read. "People just don't care about good manners anymore," she told Tillie. "All they want to read is either science fiction or horror," and then lowering her voice slightly, "or romance."

But Tillie cared. And even if Matt didn't want to know about things like proper place settings or how to make introductions or how to dress, Tillie did. In fact, she wanted to learn everything about etiquette, because one day she would live in a beautiful house like the big girl and have horses to ride. And she would fix recipes called one-dish casseroles like those described in the cooking section of MISS ANNE'S BOOK OF ETIQUETTE AND OTHER IMPORTANT THINGS instead of dirtying up a lot of pots and pans like her mom did. Because that would give her more time to ride the horses.

"Anyone going to be out today?" Evelyn asked. She spooned some yellow rice and black beans into two plastic containers for her husband and son to take with them to the fields for their mid-morning snack.

"The Big Cuban got in a fight last night," Tillie's dad answered. "Got a few stitches, but he'll be able to work.

The Big Cuban, as he was called, was their best cane cutter. He had worked in the sugarcane fields in Cuba, but had left there a few years back to work in the Florida fields for better pay. No one knew his real name. So everyone just called him the Big Cuban. Someone said he had a family in Cuba, and that as soon as he saved enough money, he was going back to them. In the meantime, he worked hard and got into fights every few weeks or so. In the four years he had worked in Capt'n Mark's fields, he had gotten one hundred twenty-four stitches, according to Tillie's addition. Tillie liked to add things. Jed Markham was the owner of Markham Farms although all the workers called him Capt'n Mark. He had talked to Tillie's dad about firing the Big Cuban.

But Dan stood up for the man, saying he was their hardest worker. He didn't drink and he didn't do drugs. He just had a lot of anger inside of him. In the end Dan was able to persuade Capt'n Mark to let him stay on. That's the way Tillie's dad was—quiet and hard-working, and willing to stand up for his men when they needed him, as long as they did right.

"There's not much wind today, so we'll burn the fields next to the north pasture," he said to Matt.

Evelyn put down two plates of eggs, smoked sausage, sliced tomatoes, and toast in front of Matt and his dad along with two big bowls of oatmeal.

"Eat it while it's hot," she said, and then she laughed. "As if anything could get cool in this weather. It must be at least 90 degrees already. And the sun is barely up."

Tillie jumped up from the table and placed a fork to the left of each of the plates her mom had put on the table along with a folded paper napkin. On the right side of the plates she laid a knife with the sharp edge facing the plate and then a spoon. After all, that's how Miss Anne would have done it. She didn't pay any attention to Matt's glare.

Meanwhile Mabe quietly ate her apple and toast, seemingly unaware of anyone else in the room. When she had finished, Tillie held up her basket in front of her.

As Mabe reached out for it, her mom quickly wiped her hands and mouth with a wet paper towel.

"That's a good girl," she said, and before Mabe could scream because she had been touched, Tillie handed her the basket. It was a routine Tillie and her mom had worked out in order to clean Mabe off each morning after breakfast before she went to school.

"The van's here." Dan stood up and went to the door.

"Finally," said Matt impatiently, as though anxious to get rid of Mabe.

But Mabe had seen it, too. With her basket in one hand and her spread under her arm, she walked with her mother to where the van was waiting at the end of the gravel drive.

"Good bye, Mabe," Tillie waved from the door.

Matt just kept eating. Sometimes it really bothered Tillie the way Matt ignored Mabe. But she didn't want to say anything that might start a ruckus. Not today.

Instead, Tillie put her empty oatmeal bowl and glass in the sink and quickly washed them. After she dried them and put them away, she picked up her book and went outside.

"Don't wander off too far, Tillie," called her mother. "I need you to help me with the wash this morning."

Tillie knew her mom needed help with the wash. Matt and her dad had to wear two pairs of pants, long-sleeved shirts over their tee-shirts, and bandannas to cover their faces and necks each day when they went into the fields in order to protect their skin from the sticky gum of the burned cane and the hot sun. So with all of that and everything else in the house that needed to be laundered, Tillie's mom always had a big wash, and it was Tillie's job to help hang it on the clotheslines outside to dry.

"I won't be long," answered Tillie. Holding tightly to her book so she wouldn't drop it, she skipped down the dirt path leading to the fields next to the big house. That was where the big girl lived with her father, Capt'n Mark, when she wasn't away at boarding school. And she was coming home today.

* * *

Matt dropped out of high school the day he turned sixteen. He just quit going. Even when he was in school, he never did his homework assignments, and he cut as many classes as he could get away with. He hated being around the other kids with all their fancy clothes and their grandiose ideas about going to college. All he wanted to do was mark time until he turned sixteen so he could start working in the sugarcane fields and make some money. "There will be plenty of time later to make money," his dad had argued. "You need to get your education first."

The guidance counselor had agreed. "You are bright," she told Matt, "but you need to apply yourself and work on your attitude." What did she know? There was no way he could study at home with Mabe the way she was—acting like a zombie one minute and a screaming maniac the next. She was fourteen years old, and she still wet her pants. She couldn't talk, she didn't understand anything that was going on, and besides that, she walked funny—always tilted to the left.

Matt had watched his mom get old and tired because of Mabe, and it had made him angry. He could remember when his mom had once been pretty, and fixed herself up with makeup, and laughed a lot. Then when Mabe came along, all that changed. She quit fixing up, her hair turned gray, and she stopped laughing. Matt couldn't remember the last time he had seen his mom wear lipstick. She probably didn't even have any.

And then there was Tillie, wandering around in a dream world of her own with that stupid book, reminding everyone about their manners. Who did she think she was anyway? Always putting on airs like she was somebody. An eleven-year-old somebody.

When Matt was younger, he had gone to the sugar-cane fields with his dad on the weekends. Dan was a cane cutter then and a good one. But instead of changing jobs and moving from one farm to another like so many of the other cane cutters, he had stayed on at Markham Farms. He liked Jed Markham and the way he ran things. Eventually, he had been given other responsibilities and more pay. He had also been allowed to move his family from the mobile home park on the edge of town where the other cane cutters with families lived into a house with a nice yard located on Markham Farms. It wasn't a big house. But with Matt, Tillie and Mabe sharing the loft that had been converted into two small bedrooms and bathroom, it was big enough.

Now Dan was cut foreman, and it was his job to make sure the cane got cut when it was supposed to. Each morning after looking over the fields, he checked on his men to see who wasn't going to be able to show up for the bus ride to whichever field needed cutting that day. The workers liked Dan Turpning. Because he had cut cane, they knew he understood what a tough job it was. And he was fair—always there to help one of them out of trouble if he needed it. And usually someone did, especially on the weekends. Dan was one of them, and as proof of it, he always carried his cane knife and wore the aluminum protective shields like the other cutters wore so he could lend a hand in the fields.

Matt had seen the way the workers looked up to his dad. He was going to work hard like his dad so one day he would be made a cut foreman. Then he would have enough money to get a place of his own to live and drive a nice truck. Maybe he'd buy his mom some makeup or a new dress.

So, against his parents' wishes and the advice of the guidance counselor, he quit school and started working in the sugarcane fields. There was a lot to learn about cutting cane, and at first Matt left too many tops and too much stubble. He was slow, and sometimes he just got in the way. His palms got so sore and callused, he had to keep them covered with Ben Gay and wintergreen oil. The other cutters made fun of him, calling him names like "*chupa-medias*." In Spanish that meant sock-sucker. They had a lot of peculiar phrases like that. Because he was the foreman's son, the other workers thought he wouldn't work hard or he would make excuses to get out of work. But Matt kept at it until he finally learned just how to lift the knife blade in order to cut a stalk of cane with one whack. Now, after a little over a year, he could cut and stack cane as fast as the best of them.

The cutters still made fun of him, though. Especially the Big Cuban. For that reason Matt always did more than was expected of him. And at the end of the day when the other workers began lining up for the bus to take them back to their barracks or their mobile homes, Matt was still in the field, cutting and stacking a few more stalks of cane. Maybe it was because he wanted the money. But more than that, more than earning the money that would get him a fancy truck and a place of his own to live or a new dress for his mom, he wanted to prove that one day he could earn some respect—like the respect he saw the other cane workers had for his dad. At least that's what he thought he wanted.

But then he met Mustafa. Mustafa introduced him to a whole new culture and made him think about things he had never thought about before. He had only attended a few of the prayer meetings, but he had learned enough to know that there was a lot more to life than cutting cane. Maybe he didn't have it so figured out after all.

"We have a lot to get done today, and it's not going to get done if we keep sitting here." Dan swallowed the last of his coffee and got up from the table. Matt followed his dad outside and climbed into the old truck. The most rows of cane he had cut in a single day were seven. Maybe today, if the sun didn't get too hot, he could cut eight. He strapped the protective shields onto his hands, preparing for the hard work ahead of him.

* * *

Mabe sat on her spread, completely still, strapped in her seat by a harness and seat belt. She held her basket tightly in her lap with both hands. Her seat, the one she always sat in, was next to a window, but she didn't look out as the van sped along the highway.

Noises from the other kids in the van assaulted her space, crossing the boundary of her spread: brown, clucking noises; green word noises; dark purple scraping noises. The noises made her skin hurt. Mabe concentrated on the seat in front of her. There was a three-inch tear across the top of the seat, and something white and fuzzy looking was sticking out. Mabe wanted to touch the white stuff—to poke her fingers down into its softness. But she didn't dare take her hands off her basket.

The kid strapped in the seat next to her had once tried to take her basket. He grabbed at it and pulled until her basket made ugly black sounds. She had screamed and screamed until she couldn't hear the ugly black sounds any more. Now she always kept both hands on her basket—holding it, protecting it.

Soon the van would stop, and Mabe would be able to get out. She would go into her school and sit on her spread in her corner with her basket—away from the ugly-colored sounds. Perhaps today she would draw the seat with the tear in it. And the white, fuzzy stuff.

Today was Thursday. She would eat chocolate chip cookies—pink sounds.

Today was Thursday. There would be music—silver sounds.

Today was Thursday. The big girl comes home to-day.

The ugly-colored sounds in the van started to fade. A pastel yellow softly and gradually settled around Mabe, soothing, caressing, filling in the gaps and spaces—blocking out the ugly colors.

Chapter Three

Tillie didn't know very much about the big girl. She had never met her. And, she supposed, she never would. After all, the big girl was older than Tillie and she wasn't at home very much, except during the summer. Last summer when the big girl got home, Tillie had asked her mom if she could go over to the big house and introduce herself. After all, she knew how to do it. She had just learned it in her book. But her mom had told her it wouldn't be proper, even if she did know how to introduce herself. So Tillie stayed away, satisfying her curiosity by occasionally catching a peek of the girl from her secret hiding place. She had overheard her dad say one time that the mother had died when Melissa was young and that an aunt had moved in to help take care of her. Tillie supposed that was why she went to a boarding school in Palm Beach. Capt'n Mark was always busy with things. When he wasn't concerned with the sugarcane business, he was traveling around buying horses to add to his already large stable of jumpers.

Tillie loved watching the horses. Every day she would go to her favorite hiding place among the stalks of wild virgin cane and Napier grass and watch them.

Sometimes, when she sat real still, they would come up and graze right next to her. She especially liked the horse named Arabesque. Everyone knew about Arabesque. She was an equestrian champion. Stories had been written about her in the newspaper along with her picture. Another horse named Molly was usually with her because Arabesque was "high-strung, and Molly quieted her" one story had explained.

Tillie climbed through the tall, thick growth of brush into a small area that had been matted down. Facing a big white stucco two-story house on the other side of the road, she sat down cross-legged. It had been seven o'clock when she saw the car leaving from the big house earlier that morning. Tillie figured someone must be going after the girl, and according to her calculations, they should be getting back in about twenty minutes. Tillie opened her book to the chapter about introductions.

"How do you do?" she said out loud. She liked the way the words sounded and felt in her mouth—sort of dressed up. That's the way etiquette was—dressed up. And when you wanted to show someone how pretty you looked, you could take it out and show it off. Not like "How ya doin'?" which was what Matt always said. Or, if he was in a good mood, which wasn't very often, he would say, "Hey! What's happnin'?" She read a little more.

"I'm very pleased to meet you," she said, tilting her head slightly. She really liked the way that sounded. Tillie repeated the words, pausing between each word. "I—am—very—pleased—to—meet—you." Then she said them very fast, running the words together. "I'mverypleasedtomeetyou."

Tillie turned the page and examined the black and white picture of a young woman, seated, leaning slightly forward, legs crossed at the ankles, extending her right hand toward a man. Printed under the picture were the words, *I am very pleased to meet you.*

Tillie uncrossed her legs and stuck them out in front of her on the crushed stalks of cane and grass. Then, placing one ankle over the other one, she leaned forward slightly and extended her right hand toward the tall, green slender leaves growing nearest her.

"I'm very pleased to meet you," she repeated once again, smiling. As she shook the leafy vegetation, she spotted a car turning off the main highway onto the blacktop road. She watched as it turned off the blacktop road and onto the gravel driveway and then park in front of the big house. In a few minutes the girl was standing on the front porch of the big house while the driver of the car unloaded seven suitcases and bags, according to Tillie's best addition. The girl was wearing faded jeans and a baggy, oversized black tee-shirt that was tied in a knot on one side. There was some sort of picture on the front of the shirt and something printed under the picture, but Tillie couldn't make it out. Tillie only managed a glimpse of the girl's hair before she disappeared into the house. It was shoulder length and slightly turned under. And she had a swing bang. At least that's what it was called in MISS ANNE'S BOOK OF ETIQUETTE AND OTHER IMPORTANT THINGS—under the chapter on personal grooming.

Tillie wished the girl had stood on the porch just a little longer so she could have seen what kind of shoes she was wearing. She watched until the driver of the car carried the last of the bags into the house. When he had finished, Tillie stood up and tied a knot in the hem of her own shirt. Then with her book in tow, she pushed her way back through the leafy stalks toward her house on the other side of the pasture.

* * *

Melissa walked through the massive double wooden front doors, crossed the marble tiled foyer, and entered the great room, as it was called. One side of the room was a wall of windows overlooking a swimming pool and the surrounding concrete deck. Beyond the pool and deck was some pasture land. And beyond that, the cane fields. Nearest the windows in one corner of the room was a black lacquered baby grand piano, her mother's piano, because this had been her mother's favorite room.

Melissa could remember sitting next to her mother at the piano with one finger resting on the note her mother had selected for her to play. As her mother played the beautiful concertos and sonatas, little Melissa had waited patiently, her finger poised on the single key, for her mother's signal. And when her mother nodded, Melissa had struck her key once and then waited again for the next signal from her mother. Often, following a series of rapid movements and difficult chords, her mother would grab up Melissa in a loving embrace, laughing about how one day they would be famous for playing the piano with two hands and one finger.

Much to her father's disappointment, it was her mother's love for music that Melissa inherited, rather than his love for horses. And as much as Melissa disliked being away from home in boarding school, at least there she was able to pursue her love of music with the best instructors.

"Aunt Joyce, I'm home," called Melissa. Immediately the clacking sound of rapid little steps on the Mexican tiled floor could be heard from another part of the large house.

"Well, there you are," announced the somewhat wiry, diminutive woman coming into the room. Aunt Joyce was the older sister of Melissa's father. She had come to Markham Farms right after Melissa's mother died in order to "help out for as long as she was needed." Eight years had passed. Melissa was now a young lady of fifteen, and Aunt Joyce was still there bustling around and "helping out."

"Let me have a good look at you," Aunt Joyce said after giving Melissa a tight hug. "You're just as pretty as ever," she said approvingly. "And now you are a high school junior. My goodness."

Melissa loved her Aunt Joyce, especially since she seemed to be blind to the fact that her niece was overweight, had zits, and wasn't very sociable because of her obtuse shyness. Or maybe Melissa loved her because she did notice those things and she just didn't act like it.

"Come out on the porch where it's cooler and have a glass of lemonade," said Aunt Joyce, pulling Melissa by the hand. Melissa glanced at the piano.

"There will be plenty of time to play the piano later," said Aunt Joyce, reading Melissa's mind. "You only just arrived. Besides, your father will be here in a few minutes, and he'll want to take you out to the stables."

"Where did he go this time?" asked Melissa, trying not to show the disappointment she felt because he hadn't picked her up from school.

"You know your father," answered Aunt Joyce. She sat down next to Melissa on a wicker settee. "He heard about a two-year-old gelding up north of here. Supposed to come from good jumper stock."

Melissa watched her aunt pour lemonade into two tall green glasses. "How are Arabesque and Molly?" she asked.

"Molly is ready to foal any day now," answered Aunt Joyce. "And Arabesque is just as nervous and high-strung as the last time you saw her. Your father thinks she will win the Gold Cup in the summer equestrian competition this year.

Melissa winced. She knew her father expected her to ride Arabesque in the competition. It was bad enough practicing the stadium jumps with only the trainer to see how terrible she was. But to perform in front of all of those people in the biggest national competition held in south Florida made her feel nervous and hungry.

Aunt Joyce patted her on the hand. "Don't worry about it," she said. "It will work out."

Just then they heard the front door slam and the unmistakable heavy trod of Jed Markham.

"Where is everybody?" he yelled.

"Out here," answered Aunt Joyce laughing. "And wipe those boots of yours before you spread horse manure all over the house," she scolded.

"A little manure is good for the house," teased the tall, middle-aged man walking out onto the porch. "Makes it smell good." Jed laughed and hugged his daughter before sitting down in the chair facing her. The smell of outdoors and horses clung to his clothing and the light, open porch seemed to shrink in the expansiveness and exuberance of Jed Markham's personality.

"When did you get home?" he asked. Aunt Joyce poured some lemonade into another glass and handed it to him.

"Just a few minutes ago," Melissa answered. She wanted to tell him how hurt she felt because he hadn't taken the time to pick her up at school. And how when all the other parents showed up for Open House, she had to hang out with her roommate's family because he was too busy to be there. And about how she had lied to her roommates about losing weight so they wouldn't know how much she really did eat when she felt lonely and unhappy. And how she still cried sometimes at night because she missed her mother so much. But Melissa didn't say any of those things. Her father wouldn't understand anyway.

"Did you find another horse?" she asked instead.

"You bet," he answered stretching his long legs out in front of him obviously pleased. "Finish your drink and I'll show him to you. A well-bred horse, comes from good Irish lines. Strong." Melissa listened to her dad telegraph the familiar phrases that she had heard all of her life. "I'm going to name him Iredale," he continued. "I think he's going to be as good as Arabesque with the proper training." He stood up, obviously impatient to show the new horse to his daughter.

Melissa put her glass down and followed her father out the door and down the drive toward the stables. As they approached the barn, Tom, the head groomsman, ran out of Molly's stall. Doc followed closely behind him carrying his big black medical bag, frowning.

"Molly's gone!" both men yelled in unison.

Chapter Four

Matt struck hard at the cane stalk and continued moving down the row at a faster pace than normal. Meeting Abdullah had stirred up more questions. The fundamentals of the Muslim faith were good as far as he could tell. There was *sahah*, or daily prayer, *ibadah*, which was submission to Allah or God. *Zalsah* was paying 2.5 percent of his salary to a deserving fellow being—his parents called it tithing. There was fasting during the month of Ramadin or ninth month. And there was *hajj*, or pilgrimage, to Mecca. This was considered the biggest of all acts of worship. It was where Muslims from around the world were united into one international brotherhood. Mustafa talked a lot about the hajj. It was his hope to go some time in the next year. He had even suggested that Matt go with him—that is, if he decided to convert to Islam.

The prayer and worship and giving to others were all good things as far as Matt was concerned. He didn't have much to give, but he wouldn't mind sharing it. Abdullah had made a special point to single him out after the meeting, telling him that he had heard good things about him. That the "Brotherhood" needed good men like him. That was when Abdullah invited him to a special meeting they were having later in the week. Abdullah had actually called him a man. He had also told him that if he needed anything to let him know. "It is an honor," Mustafa had told him later, "for Abdullah to take special notice."

Matt felt good. He liked his new friends and he liked what he was learning about Islam. Abdullah was a leader. Matt noticed how much everyone looked up to him—respected him. That was what he wanted, too. Respect. But being the son of a cut foreman who worked in a cane field brought on more jokes than respect from the other workers.

Matt straightened up from his stooped position and wiped the sweat from his face. Behind him lay hundreds of long cane stalks neatly cut and piled in a row. *The Brotherhood needs good men like you.* He would attend the special meeting even if it did mean sneaking out of the house.

* * *

Tillie skipped through the green, uncut grass of the pasture toward the border of trees that separated the grazing land from the field of sugarcane. Butterflies, bees, and an occasional dragonfly buzzed around her.

The sky was a bright orange, and the air smelled like a mixture of cotton candy and roasted corn from the burning field of cane nearby. Tillie began running. She knew her mom would be expecting her. When she approached the nearest thicket of trees, something moved in the tall grass in front of her, causing Tillie to jump with fright. There, lying on the ground in front of her was a horse. It was the horse Tillie had seen pictured in the paper with Arabesque. It was Molly.

"How do you do?" said Tillie as she cautiously walked up to the horse. Molly jerked her head up nervously and snorted loudly through her nostrils. Tillie tried to remember everything she had ever read about animals and, in particular, horses, in MISS ANNE'S BOOK OF ETIQUETTE AND OTHER IMPORTANT THINGS. *Gently blow into the horse's nostrils so that it will become familiar with your scent.* She kneeled down in front of Molly, putting her book aside in the grass.

"I'm very pleased to meet you, Molly," she said, blowing gently toward the horse's nose. Molly's ears perked up at the mention of her name. Then she nuzzled the girl's face and neck, smelling her airs, her skin, her hair, and her clothes. Tillie sat quietly, allowing Molly's nose and mouth to explore her. When Molly was at last satisfied that this girl who smelled like warm oats, sugar, and grass was not a threat, she whinnied and lay her head back on the soft grass.

Tillie reached out and stroked Molly. "Where is Arabesque?" Tillie asked, glancing around for the other horses. But there were no other horses in sight. "What's the matter, Molly?" asked Tillie softly. "Can't you get up?"

Molly's eyes grew wide with fright, and she kicked her hind legs while screeching terribly from deep within her throat. Startled, Tillie fell back, and when she did, she saw what was happening. Molly was getting ready to foal. And she was getting ready now! Tillie looked toward the big house, but she couldn't see it. The wind had changed direction, and already a thick heavy smoke from the burning cane field was starting to spread a black oily soot around them.

"I'll go get help, Molly," said Tillie, wiping her stinging eyes with the knot tied in her shirt. But before she could get up, Molly let out the loud screeching noise again and began thrashing her hind legs on the ground as though in pain.

Tillie moved up closer to Molly and continued talking to her, stroking her neck and stomach, trying to calm her. Something was wrong. One little hoof and leg was protruding from the birth canal, but it seemed to be stuck. Tillie didn't know anything about animals giving birth. The closest she had ever come to it was when her sixth-grade school class went on a field trip to a chicken farm. There the kids got to see an egg hatch. Afterwards, each of the kids had been given a baby chick to take care of in the classroom as a sort of science project. Tillie had tied a piece of red ribbon around the leg of her chick so she could tell it apart from all the others. But the other chicks kept pecking at the ribbon until they made her chick's leg bleed. So she had to take the ribbon off. She said she could still tell her chick from the rest because her chick had a mean look in his eye. Probably from getting pecked at so much.

But this was different—a lot different. Tillie continued to stroke Molly not wanting to break the connection between her and the distressed animal. Carefully Tillie moved behind her, talking softly the whole time and watching Molly's powerful back legs in case they kicked again.

"It's all right, Molly," she said. "You are going to have a beautiful foal. Arabesque will be so proud of you." Tillie kept talking while feeling for the other small hoof and leg. It was twisted the wrong way and preventing the birth to take place. Tillie's eyes were stinging from the smoke and she wiped them again. With a trembling hand she slowly reached beyond the exposed leg and carefully straightened the other one that was twisted. When she did, Molly's stomach contracted one last time and the new foal was born.

Tillie reached for the clean hanky she had stuffed into her pocket earlier that morning and tenderly wiped the newborn's nostrils, mouth, and eyes clear of any mucus and bits of membrane from the birth. Then she blew softly into the small horse's face.

"How do you do, little foal," she said. Struggling with its weight, she carefully picked up the new-born horse and placed it in front of Molly. Tillie blew one more time at Molly and her new foal just to make sure they recognized her as a friend. "I'm so very pleased to meet you, little foal," said Tillie. But the little foal didn't pay any attention. He was already enjoying the gentle nudges and lickings of his mother's tongue.

Tillie looked on for just a moment longer to make sure that the young foal and its mother were all right. Then she began running across the pasture in the direction of the big house as fast as her legs would carry her. When a wild rabbit jumped in front of Tillie trying to escape the dense smoke, Tillie stumbled and fell, cutting her knee and scraping her shin. But she got up and began running again. Her chest ached from breathing the black smoke, and when she looked back, she couldn't see Molly or the colt. The smoke had already closed in around them. Tillie tried to run faster. Blood dripped from her leg onto her sneaker and tears streamed down her cheeks as she tried to see her way through the thick smoke. When she got closer to the big house, she could see some men and the girl talking in the stable yard. She climbed over the corral fence and ran down the gravel drive to where they were.

"Molly's just had a foal!" she panted. She bent over nearly collapsing in exhaustion, her lungs hurting and her eyes stinging from the smoke and sweat.

Jed Markham grabbed her arm. "Where is she?"

"Across the pasture," Tillie said, gasping for breath and looking in the direction she had just come from, "in a clump of trees."

"Show us," he said. "We'll take the pickup. Tom, throw a couple of hay bales in the back. You and Doc ride back there, and she'll ride in front with me," he ordered, pulling Tillie toward the cab of the truck. He yanked the door of the truck open and pushed Tillie in. As Tom loaded the hay, Doc grabbed his medical bag and shoved it into the truck. Eyes wide with fright, Melissa stood silently watching as they all climbed into the truck.

"You too, Melissa," shouted her father. "Ride up here."

Quickly Melissa climbed in next to Tillie. Tillie noticed she was wearing clean white sneakers with lace shoestrings. The picture on her tee-shirt, the one she had been unable to see from her special hiding place, was of a man with funny-looking long hair. *Mozart* was the word printed under the picture. Miss Anne would have said that Melissa looked casually sophisticated, thought Tillie.

Tillie's own clothes were soaked with sweat and blood from the birth and from her own scraped leg, and she couldn't stop trembling. Jed sped through the bumpy, open pasture, throwing Tillie from side to side in the cab of the truck.

"Up there in those trees," pointed Tillie. Unable to hold herself steady, she tried to wipe her eyes with the sleeve of her shirt without being too obvious about it. After all, it wasn't a very lady-like thing to do.

When the pickup stopped, the other men jumped out and ran over to where Molly was now standing and still licking her brand new foal. Jed, Melissa, and Tillie watched while Doc checked over the foal and its mother. Meanwhile Tom began spreading the two bales of hay, making a soft bed in the back end of the truck.

"Tell me about the birth, young lady," said Doc.

Tillie explained how only one leg had come out because the other one was somehow twisted. She told him how she was able to straighten the twisted leg and when the foal was born, how she had wiped its face with her clean hanky. She held up her hanky to show him. "Then I blew into his face to introduce myself so he would know I was a friend," Tillie added.

"Well, he's as good as new," said Doc chuckling at his own joke. "Not a thing wrong with him as far as I can tell. Or Molly either. Where did you learn so much about horses?" he asked suddenly.

"I really don't know anything about them," said Tillie honestly, "except that I love them and, of course, what I have read in MISS ANNE'S BOOK OF ETIQUETTE AND OTHER IMPORTANT THINGS. Although once I had a baby chicken," she added.

"Well, you did a fine job here," he smiled.

Tillie stuffed her soiled hanky back into her pocket. "I'd better go home now," she said. "I have to help my mom with the wash." And then remembering her manners, "Thank you."

"What's your name?" asked Jed.

"Tillie," she answered, extending her hand and slightly tilting her head like she had seen the lady do in the picture of her book. "I'm Tillie, Dan Turpning's girl."

"Well, I owe you my thanks, Tillie," he said, shaking her small hand between his two big ones.

"You're welcome." Tillie turned to walk away.

"Tillie, is this yours?" Melissa picked up the tattered book off the ground and handed it to her. In all the excitement, Tillie had almost gone off and left it.

"See you later, Tillie," said Melissa.

Tillie took her most prized possession and ran through the trees toward her house in the clearing on the other side of the pasture.

* * *

The cane field was already burning when the wind shifted unexpectedly. There was nothing to do but put the fire out and move the workers to another field that had been burned earlier in the week. Dan didn't like it when this happened. For one thing it wasted a lot of time, valuable time, moving the workers from field to field. More importantly, though, when the wind blew from the west toward the east, people in the nearby towns and communities complained of the smoke and of the black soot that covered everything. He tried to avoid this as best he could, but sometimes, like today, the wind shifted while a field was burning.

"Matt, I want you to work this field with the Big Cuban while I take the other cutters to the north field." Dan always left a couple of workers in a burned field just to make sure the fire didn't start up again and to cut whatever cane was dry enough to cut. That way at least some work would get done in the field.

The Big Cuban grinned at Matt, displaying his upper front teeth framed in gold. "Eh, *chupa-medias*, you take it easy today, no?"

Matt ignored him. He was thinking about some of the things he had read in the Qur'an that didn't make a whole lot of sense to him. Maybe he could ask Abdullah about the things he didn't understand at the special meeting he had been invited to. Matt went to the far end of the field where the fire had first been set and began cutting the cane stalks. They were already dry from the heat of the fire and sun. Because they had to change fields, he was getting a late start. He might be able to cut three rows before his dad returned to check on his progress. He would be ready for his mid-morning snack by then too. Then after that, if he didn't take a break, maybe he could cut five more, making a total of eight rows. He glanced up from his cutting and saw the Big Cuban walking along the fire line, spreading ashes with his feet and blade. If he worked hard, he still might even be able to cut nine rows.

Chapter Five

The exhilaration and happiness Tillie felt was almost overwhelming. She remembered how one of her teachers always spoke of special events in history as being "red-letter days" because they were memorable or of some special significance. Tillie didn't have a calendar, but if she did have one, she would definitely have circled the day's date in red. And she would have drawn a smiley face on it the way her teacher did when she handed in a good homework assignment.

When Tillie walked into her yard, her mom was hanging up the wash on the clothesline to dry, and Mabe was already home from school. She was sitting on her spread under a large ficus tree sketching the laundry basket. Or at least that's what it looked like to Tillie.

"Tillie, where have you been so long?" asked her mother, straightening up from the basket heaped with wet clothes. And then seeing the mess Tillie was in, "Look at you! What in the world did you get into?" Fear filled her eyes. "Are you all right?" she gasped rushing over to her youngest child.

"I know I'm late, Mama," said Tillie. "But wait until I tell you what happened."

Evelyn listened to Tillie tell her about Molly and how she had helped the new foal be born, and about meeting Capt'n Mark and Melissa. "I would have crossed my ankles when I shook their hands, the way it showed in the book, but I was standing up, so I guess it was all right that I didn't." Then she told her mom about how Doc had said she had done a good job and about how in all the excitement she had almost left her book behind, but the big girl—Melissa—found it and gave it back to her.

"You did a very wonderful and brave thing," Evelyn told her young daughter holding her at a distance to examine her to make sure she wasn't hurt. Then she put her arms around her and drew her close. "There is nothing more wonderful than witnessing a new life come into this world." She wrapped her arms around Tillie and kissed the top of her head. "Your dad and Matt will be coming home for lunch soon. You'd better go wash up and change clothes. I'll finish hanging out the wash."

Later, when they were all sitting around the kitchen table eating lunch, Tillie once more told her story about Molly and the new foal.

"You're lucky you didn't get kicked in the head," said Matt, feeling a little jealous of the attention Tillie was getting.

Molly wouldn't have hurt me," said Tillie, smoothing the clean white bandages her mom had put over her cuts and scrapes. "Not after I introduced myself."

Matt shook his head and kept eating. Just then a pickup truck pulled into the yard and stopped. Dan got up to see who it was. "It's Capt'n Mark," he said, and opened the screen door. Jed Markham and Melissa entered the small kitchen.

"We were just having lunch," said Evelyn. "Won't you have some with us?" This was the first time Capt'n Mark and his daughter had visited them at home, and she felt a little flustered. She really didn't have enough food prepared for two extra people, but she would make do.

"No, thank you, Mrs. Turpning," answered Jed. "We won't be staying. It smells mighty good, though," he added.

Matt had stood up when Capt'n Mark and his daughter walked into the kitchen and was now, Tillie was pleased to see, offering his chair to Melissa. Melissa didn't sit down, but at least Matt offered. Dan continued standing, quietly waiting for Capt'n Mark to explain the purpose of his visit. Evelyn briskly wiped her hands on the apron tied around her waist, even though her hands were already dry. Tillie stood next to her dad holding her breath, afraid that introducing herself to Molly and the new foal hadn't been such a good thing after all, afraid something had happened to the new little foal or Molly. Only Mabe seemed unruffled by this highly unusual visit and continued rocking rhythmically in her chair while moving a square of buttered cornbread around on her plate with her finger.

"Dan." Jed Markham's voice seemed to fill the entire house. "Your daughter did a fine, brave thing for us this morning. We might have lost a valuable horse and her foal if it hadn't been for Tillie's quick thinking. And I am indebted to her."

Tillie started breathing again, and her dad put his arm around her. Matt kept ogling Melissa, and Evelyn smiled.

"I understand she likes horses," he continued, looking at Tillie. Without waiting for a response, he said, "My daughter, Melissa, resumes her training sessions tomorrow in stadium jumping. I want to invite Tillie to join her. She can learn as much as she wants about riding horses."

Tillie held her breath again. To be able to ride a horse—especially one of Capt'n Mark's horses—was better than anything she had ever dreamed of.

"It won't cost you. I'll take care of everything," he said. "And if she's as good with horses as I think she is, she'll be able to compete with others in the Youth

Division for the Equestrian Gold Cup at the end of the summer. It would be a good experience for her, and I think she'd like it."

Tillie glanced up at her dad and then at her mom who was wiping her hands on her apron again. Her dad, as usual, was quiet, studying over Capt'n Mark's words. Mabe jammed her middle finger into the piece of cornbread and held it up in the air.

Capt'n Mark looked at Mabe. "I have plenty of help up at the house. I'd be more than happy to send one of the women down here to help Mrs. Turpning with the wash and other chores Tillie would miss by not being here." And then once more for emphasis, he said, "It won't cost you anything, Dan. In fact, you would be doing me a favor by allowing me to repay Tillie in this way for what she did."

Dan looked at his young daughter. Never had Tillie looked happier than she did at that moment. "I guess we'd better ask Tillie," he said.

All of the feelings and emotions Tillie had been holding back suddenly erupted. She bolted toward the man who had just granted one of her grandest, most secret wishes.

"Oh, thank you, Capt'n Mark," she said, once more taking his hand and shaking it. "And thank you, Melissa," she said, thrusting her small hand into

Melissa's plump one and pumping it up and down as well.

Melissa laughed. "I'm glad you want to come," she said. "It will be a lot more fun having someone to practice with."

The Turpnings—Dan, Evelyn, Matt, and Tillie—stood on their small front porch and watched the Markham Farms pickup truck drive away. Back in the kitchen, with the cornbread still impaled on her finger, Mabe announced loudly, "The big girl gets home today."

Chapter Six

Molly shivered with happiness and contentment as her young foal nursed greedily. Even though it had been only a few hours since its birth, the foal was already standing—although somewhat shakily—and enjoying the comfort and security of his mother's stall.

Arabesque had been brought back from the north pasture and put into her stall next to Molly so she could soothe her best friend from the rigors of being a new mother. Arabesque had sniffed at length the miniature horse and Molly, trying to understand what had taken place. Except for another scent that smelled a lot like a mixture of warm oats, sugar, and grass, Molly smelled just the way she always did. And the young foal smelled a lot like Molly except for a newness about it. And it, too, had that curious scent of warm oats, sugar, and grass. It was a nice smell. It was friendly.

The foal grew weary, and as it butted his mother's udder for one last drop of milk, it almost fell down. Finally he felt satisfied, and after glancing around, he wobbled over to a corner of the stall. There in the fresh clean straw he curled up and promptly went to sleep.

And Arabesque, feeling protective toward the foal, watched over him during the night as Molly also slept.

The next morning, the man who smelled like leather, tobacco, and wild cherries entered Arabesque's stall. After feeding her some hay and a mixture of carrots, apples, and damp bran, he led her, along with another horse named King Sugar, to the paddock where he placed a saddle blanket and saddle on her back and worked the bit of a bridle into her mouth. When he had done the same thing with King Sugar, he led them both to the jumping practice area.

Arabesque didn't want to leave Molly and the foal, and she was indignant at being taken from her stall. She didn't feel like practicing jumps. She snorted loudly and pawed the ground with her front right hoof. Then she angrily switched her tail rapidly up and down in three consecutive motions.

"Feeling a little temperamental this morning, are we?" the man asked pleasantly. Arabesque reached out with her bitted mouth and tried to nip his shoulder. When she did, she spotted the girl from the big house ambling toward the practice area with a smaller girl skipping along beside her. Arabesque blew hard through her nostrils. She definitely wasn't in the mood to be ridden by the big girl. She had been ridden by the big girl for over three years now, and the big girl still didn't know how to give commands. She pressed her knees too hard into Arabesque's sides and pulled the reins too hard, causing the bit to make Arabesque's mouth sore. Not only that, she was heavy, and she always smelled nervous.

The big girl tentatively walked up to Arabesque. Arabesque glared at her and snorted. As usual the big girl smelled nervous.

"Better watch Arabesque this morning," warned Tom. "She's acting a bit testy." He locked his fingers together and lifted Melissa into the saddle. But before Melissa could take hold of the reins, Arabesque reared up on her hind legs and threw Melissa onto the ground.

Tillie ran over to help Melissa up. "Are you all right?" she asked, glancing back at Arabesque and then at the big horse standing next to her that she was supposed to ride.

"Oh, yes," said Melissa grimacing. She brushed off the seat of her riding britches. "It's not the first time I've been thrown, and I suppose it won't be the last."

After three more attempts, Melissa finally was able to mount Arabesque. And Tillie, sitting astride King Sugar, began her first lesson in horseback riding.

JULY

Chapter Seven

How doth the little busy bee
Improve each shining hour,
And gather honey all the day
From every opening flower!

Tillie sang the little ditty she had memorized from MISS ANNE'S BOOK OF ETIQUETTE AND OTHER IMPORTANT THINGS as she busily washed the breakfast dishes. Mabe had already left for school, and Matt and his dad were still sitting at the table discussing a problem that had come up during the night. The Big Cuban had gotten into another fight—twenty-five stitches—and would have to be out for at least three days. Dan and the other workers normally could make up the slack, but the west field that ran along the canal had already been burned earlier in the week, and the cane needed to be cut. It was also the largest field.

"Let me work the Charlie Frank row until the Big Cuban gets back, Dad," said Matt. The Charlie Frank row was what the workers called the row of cane bordering the canal and edge of the field. It was more difficult to cut than the rest, but it also paid more. Always before, the Big Cuban had cut it. Matt watched his dad blow into the steaming mug of coffee he was holding. "I'll do it right."

Dan put the mug back on the table and studied it. Matt didn't say anything else. His dad knew better than anyone what kind of cutter he was. If he felt he was ready for the Charlie Frank row, he would tell him.

"We had some wind yesterday, so there will be some rooster tail in it," his dad said.

Matt knew only too well the difficulty in cutting cane twisted by the wind. The first cane he ever tried to cut was rooster tail cane. "I'll do it right," he repeated.

Tillie picked up Matt's breakfast plate, placing the dirty fork and knife across the plate with the handles pointing outward, and carried it to the sink to wash. Normally Matt would have complained about her putting on airs, but he was concentrating too hard on his dad's face to notice.

"Is your bill sharp?" asked Dan, referring to Matt's cane knife. He glanced up from his coffee mug toward his son. Matt had been more withdrawn and irritable than usual the past few weeks. It probably had something to do with his sneaking out at night. He had heard some of the workers talking about a new "element" who had settled nearby. Unlike the Muslims who had been living and working in that area for years and got along with everyone—good, honest folks—this new group seemed to be looking for trouble. Matt was hardheaded. He proved that when he dropped out of school. He had been taught right from wrong, and he usually did the right thing. But he needed to learn his own lessons. Dan just hoped his son wasn't mixed up in something that would get him hurt in the process.

"Sharpened it last night."

Dan nodded. Maybe giving him some extra responsibility would help bring him out of whatever was bothering him.

Matt knew he had gotten what he wanted. His dad was going to let him take over the Big Cuban's job. Now he would show everyone just how good he was.

"They burned the south field yesterday near where you'll be cutting, so watch out for the fire ants and snakes," said Matt's dad. "And they'll be burning the field east of there this morning. It's dry and no wind, so there shouldn't be much smoke. If a wind does pick up, though, and starts blowing toward the canal, you'll need to get out of there fast."

"Yes, sir," said Matt still grinning.

Evelyn finished wiping off the stove. She didn't say anything. Matt had been cutting cane for almost two years now. The decision of where he should cut was between him and his dad. She never interfered in decisions involving the cane fields.

As soon as Matt got to the field, he took off walking toward the canal. Two other men who were assigned to work the row next to the Charlie Frank row followed behind. Matt didn't waste any time. He immediately began cutting the stalks of cane and laying them on the ground to be picked up later. It was difficult sorting the cane from the tangle of weeds that grew up from the canal bank. Matt had never worked so hard in his life. His dad already knew how good he was, but this was his chance to prove how good he was to the others so they wouldn't think of him as being a *chupa-medias*. Two hours after he started cutting he was already ahead of the other two men working the next row over. It was hot, and there was no breeze. His clothes were wet with sweat. But he was used to it. When the whistle blew calling the workers to the north end of the field for their mid-morning break, Matt only took long enough to drink some water and grab a piece of cornbread. Then back to his row he went, cutting and stacking the stalks of cane.

At lunch break, again he only took enough time to drink some water and quickly eat a bowl of stew. Then, while the other workers rested, he went back to the field. He was so intent on finishing, he didn't notice when a slight westerly breeze started to stir. A few minutes later when the breeze started to gust, Matt only noticed that he was three-quarters of the way down the Charlie Frank row. If he kept working at the same pace, he could finish it by nightfall. Even the Big Cuban hadn't been able to do that. It always took him at least a day and a half.

Matt's eyes started to sting. When he stopped to rub them on his bandanna, it was then that he noticed the smoke. The fire that had been set in the other field had spread into the stalks of cane next to where he was cutting. It quickly skirted the outer fringe of the field, fed by the brisk wind. The thick black smoke was suffocating, and Matt couldn't see. He tried running back along the row where he had just finished cutting, but new flames blocked his passage. The sound of the crackling fire burning the stalks was almost deafening. Somewhere in the distance he thought he could hear his dad yelling for him, but he couldn't make out which direction the sound was coming from.

Matt tried to cut across the field, through the rows of uncut cane. But the fire closed in once again. He felt like he was choking. He pulled off the bandanna from around his neck and tied it over his face. Then, helplessly, he got down on his hands and knees and began crawling slowly back toward the Charlie Frank row. The uncut cane scratched and bruised his legs and arms. Fire ants bit his bare skin. But he held his head down and kept crawling. He didn't dare stop.

* * *

Mabe sat in a large green upholstered chair in Dr. Harrison's office. It felt soft to her back and legs. It was nice. It sounded violet. Her spread was bunched up under her arm, and her basket rested in her lap.

"And who is this?" asked Dr. Harrison. He held up a photograph in front of Mabe. This was part of a weekly instruction class to help Mabe recognize and associate the photographs she was shown with members of her family.

"Tillie rides horses," Mabe said, looking at the picture.

"That's good, Mabe." Dr. Harrison smiled. "This is a picture of Tillie."

"Tillie rides horses," Mabe repeated.

"And who is this?" asked Dr. Harrison, holding up a photograph of Matt.

"Matt works," said Mabe.

"Good, Mabe," said Dr. Harrison. "This is a picture of Matt. Who is Matt?" he asked.

"Matt works," said Mabe.

"All right, Mabe. Now tell me who this is." Dr. Harrison held up a picture of Mabe's mother.

"Uh huh," said Mabe. She reached into her basket and started fidgeting with the broken crayons.

"Mabe, look at this picture and tell me who it is," Dr. Harrison repeated, using the same gentle tone of voice he had used earlier.

"Uh huh," said Mabe.

Dr. Harrison picked up another picture, this one of Mabe's father.

"Who is this, Mabe?" he asked.

But Mabe was no longer concentrating. A sort of tan color had crept into the room and was moving closer to where she was sitting. It was making her feel uneasy, because sometimes tan turned dark brown and then black. Black was loud and it hurt.

"Uh huh," she said again without having been asked anything. Her fingers became more agitated, picking up first one crayon and then another in her basket. And then she began rocking back and forth.

"That's all right, Mabe," said Dr. Harrison. "I think we've done enough for today."

He pushed a button on his desk signaling the outer office. A woman entered the room.

"All finished now?" she asked cheerfully and she walked over to where Mabe was sitting.

Mabe stood up and gathered her spread and basket into her arms. The tan color was starting to go away again. Mabe paused, watching and listening, just to make sure. Then she followed the woman out the door.

* * *

Later that evening, Matt sat in the middle of the living room on a chair that had been brought from the kitchen. His dad, mom, and Tillie sat on the couch listening as he told them for the third time how he had barely managed to escape the fire. Mabe sat on her spread on the floor in a corner, drawing with a red crayon what looked like the legs of the chair on which Matt was sitting. Even though it was still early and it wasn't quite dark outside yet, Matt was already in his pajamas. The only physical evidence of his terrifying experience was a few scratches on his arms and legs, and some large red splotches on his shoulders that would more than likely turn into purple bruises in a day or two. Also, one foot was heavily coated with a white ointment that was supposed to keep the fire ant bites from itching so much.

"Then, when I realized that the fire was all around me, I did the only thing I could. I crawled my way back to the Charlie Frank row and jumped into the canal."

Dan shook his head. "That wind blew up in such a hurry, no one even saw it coming. It only lasted about fifteen minutes, but when I think of what could have happened."

Evelyn took her husband's hand. "Well, we won't dwell on that," she said softly.

"By the way," Dan smiled at his son with pride. "Capt'n Mark said your row was the best cutting job he had ever seen."

Matt grunted. "I would have finished it, too, if it hadn't been for the fire."

"There's always tomorrow, Matt," said his dad.

Mabe got up from her spread with the picture she had been drawing and walked over to Matt. She tilted to the left the way she always did when she walked, but her eyes were bright and focused. She handed Matt the picture, which wasn't chair legs at all, but a field with rows of cut and uncut sugarcane colored in red. She rested her cheek on Matt's head.

"Brebe," she said. And then she went back to her spread and sat down. Her face was expressionless. She was once more locked in the security of a secret, distant place that only she knew.

Matt turned away, tears rolling down his cheeks. During the whole ordeal he hadn't cried. Now that everything was all right and he was safe, he was acting like a little baby. He knocked his tears away brusquely and sniffed loudly. Dan put his arm around his wife, bracing for the onslaught of emotion that was bound to come from that direction as well. His own eyes grew moist. Only Tillie acted with calm. She jumped up and handed Matt the clean hanky she pulled from her pocket.

"Miss Anne says a gentleman should keep a hanky in his coat breast pocket for looks and another one in his hip pants pocket for utility."

This is quite a family, thought Matt, not trusting his voice to say it out loud. Strangely enough, even with all of his ant bites and bruises and scrapes, he felt good. The anger and frustration that had been his companions for so long had somehow diminished—just like the smoke of the burning cane.

Chapter Eight

From that very first day Tillie loved everything about horseback riding, just as she had always known she would. Each morning she would wake up early, dress, and then watch impatiently for the first signs of daylight. It was midsummer now, and the heat was so oppressive that her mom had to keep the wooden slatted shutters on the windows closed in order to block the hot penetrating rays of the sun. On the shutters covering the loft window of Tillie's and Mabe's bedroom, however, two of the slats were wider apart than the others thereby forming a gap she could see through. And it was on this gap that Tillie focused her attention each morning. When the first streaks of light glimmered between those two slats, she knew she could get up and dress without disturbing the rest of her family. And after helping her mom get Mabe ready for school and eating breakfast, she would head for the stables, carrying MISS ANNE'S BOOK OF ETIQUETTE AND OTHER IMPORTANT THINGS with her.

Melissa usually slept late, and the trainer didn't get to the stables before nine each morning. But Tillie would go to the pasture where Molly and her foal, which

Capt'n Mark had named Markette, were grazing and read to them from her book until it was time for her riding lesson.

King Sugar wasn't as grand as Arabesque or as quick, but he was a handsome golden color, and he tried hard; and he didn't seem to mind if Tillie made a mistake. After just a few lessons, Tillie had already mastered how to sit in the saddle and hold the reins properly for posting. She could walk, cantor, trot, and gallop King Sugar without bouncing all over the horse's back. She learned how to use only the slightest pressure with her knees and legs, or tension on the reins, to signal King Sugar her instructions. And when she did, King Sugar expertly maneuvered his powerful body through the difficult movements just as he was commanded.

A few weeks later, when she began her training in stadium jumping, Tillie quickly learned how to use her own weight to help King Sugar negotiate the barriers and hazards, shifting her body to correspond with his. If King Sugar balked or knocked over one of the barricades, Tillie would go back and start over from the beginning until she got it right. For she felt that the mistake had been her fault for miscommunicating to King Sugar. The stadium jumps were Tillie's favorite. She loved the feeling of flying freely through the air, of turning King Sugar toward a barrier and knowing that he was ready for it by the way he perked his ears forward and tensed his large muscular body.

More than anything else, Tillie was glad to have Melissa for a friend. Melissa's life was so different from Tillie's. But Melissa made Tillie feel comfortable and welcomed—inviting her into the big house and sharing her music and her Aunt Joyce with her. And they talked. Sometimes about nothing in particular. Or, at other times, about school and the people they knew. One of Melissa's roommates from school wrote to her every week—sometimes twice a week, and Melissa even let Tillie read the letters. And then there were those special times when no one else was around to listen that they would talk about how one day Melissa was going to be a famous concert pianist and Tillie was going to be a grand lady living in a big house with lots of beautiful horses like Arabesque and Molly and King Sugar and the little foal.

* * *

Melissa despised going to the stables each morning. It was all she could do to force herself to get up and dress and eat the breakfast her Aunt Joyce had prepared for her. If it hadn't been for Tillie being there, she would have refused to go. But she really liked Tillie, even if she was a little peculiar and even if she did drag around that decrepit old book everywhere. Tillie was always so cheerful and enthusiastic about everything. Melissa had never known anyone who found so much pleasure in so little. Sometimes, after they finished their riding lessons, they would help Tom groom Arabesque and King Sugar. Then Melissa would invite Tillie into the great room of her house and play the piano for her. No matter what Melissa played, or how often she played it, when she finished Tillie would stand up clapping her hands and say "Brava." She had learned about it in that book she carried around.

The more proficient Tillie became in her equestrian training, the more frustrating it was for Melissa. It was just so easy for Tillie. And even though Melissa had been taking lessons for several years now, she couldn't seem to get it right. She knew the trainer was growing impatient with her for not settling down and concentrating. And Melissa was positive she could see Arabesque wince whenever it was her turn to do the jumps. Sometimes Melissa would see her father watching the sessions from the fence. He couldn't be pleased with her progress. In fact, the only good thing that had come out of all of it, besides having Tillie for a friend, was that she was losing weight. Melissa no longer sneaked food to her room at night. She hadn't even wanted any snacks between meals. And it was beginning to show. Her clothes were much looser, her face was zit-free and had a healthy glow to it, she had a lot more energy, and she felt more sure of herself—at least when she wasn't riding Arabesque.

After dinner one evening Melissa was sitting at the piano practicing a piece of music she hoped to memorize. It was Chopin's *Etude in A Minor*, and it had been one of her mother's favorite pieces. Her father came into the room and sat down on the bench next to Melissa.

"I never understood your mother's love for music over horses, but I respected it," he said. "And I enjoyed listening to her play." Melissa looked up at him. He had never mentioned her mother's music before.

"The Gold Cup Competition is in a couple of weeks, as you know," he said, changing the subject. "I've been thinking about entering Tillie in the Youth Division and letting her ride Arabesque in it; that is, if you don't mind."

"Mind!" Melissa said. She held on to the edge of the piano bench and thought seriously of doing several cartwheels. "Tillie is perfect for Arabesque. She is so much better than I could ever be," she said. Melissa hugged her father. "And she can win!"

"Well, that might be, but she'll need you there for support. Competition is a frightening thing, especially when it's your first one," he said.

"Don't worry," said Melissa. "I'll be right there along with Molly and little Markette giving Tillie and Arabesque all the support they need. We'll be a regular cheering gallery."

"By the way." Melissa's father gazed out of the windows and beyond the pool. "It isn't too soon to start sending off for information from those music schools you're interested in. After all, with your talent and ability, you'll want to go to a good one after you graduate from Sweet Palms."

Melissa put her arms around her father. Maybe he did understand—at least some things. She was going to be a great pianist. And Tillie was going to ride Arabesque for the Equestrian Gold Cup—and win.

Chapter Nine

Molly ate her usual morning mixture of oats, bran, carrots, apples, and other good-tasting things. Markette slept peacefully nearby on the sweet-smelling hay in the corner of the stall. Soon she and her foal would be taken to the pasture next to where Arabesque and King Sugar practiced their jumps. There Molly would graze while her foal nursed or explored the area nearby, but never venturing too far from his mother's side.

The girl who smelled like warm oats, sugar, and grass was there every day now. She would come to the pasture early in the morning with Molly and little Markette and sit on the grass with a book in her lap. Then she would look at the book and say words to Molly and her foal. Words like, "You must never introduce people to each other in public places unless you are certain that the introduction will be agreeable to both." Or, "Don't talk or laugh loud enough to attract attention."

Molly didn't understand what the words meant, but she liked the way they sounded, and she liked the girl and her airs. The girl had helped her when she was in pain. She was her friend, like Arabesque was her friend.

While Tillie turned the pages of her book and read things out loud, Molly contentedly munched on the grass nearby. Sometimes Markette would get a sudden adventurous streak of bravery and try to take a nibble from the girl's book. This would make Tillie laugh, and when she did, the foal would bolt back to his mother where he would suck her teat.

After a while, the man who smelled like leather, tobacco, and wild cherries would bring Arabesque and King Sugar to the jumping practice area. The big girl who rode Arabesque would come too. Molly knew that Arabesque didn't like the big girl. Molly and Markette would stand by the fence separating the pasture from the jumping practice area and watch. When Arabesque completed an especially hard exercise, she would look at Molly for approval.

After they finished practicing, and after King Sugar and Arabesque had been groomed, they would be turned loose in the pasture where Molly and her foal were. Arabesque and Molly would smell one another as well as little Markette. There were all the old familiar scents and the new scent which was now a part of them. It was the scent of warm oats, sugar, and grass.

On this particular day Molly and Markette watched from the fence rail as Arabesque was led into the practice area. Then a strange thing happened. Instead of mounting Arabesque, the big girl walked over to where Molly and her foal were. The girl who smelled like warm oats, sugar, and grass was lifted onto Arabesque. For the next two hours, Arabesque and the girl negotiated the various jumps, turns, and barriers. Then they practiced cantering, trotting, walking; forward and backward; running and stopping. And then they practiced the jumps again. Not once did Arabesque miss the commands. When they finally finished, Arabesque proudly looked over at Molly. It had been a good practice session. She had performed well.

Chapter Ten

Daylight was slowly fading, making it difficult to see. The other workers had already left the field and were now loading onto the bus that would take them back to their barracks and trailers for the night. Matt had just a few more stalks of cane to cut before finishing the row. That was what he had set out to do early that morning, and he wanted to complete it.

Matt hadn't gone back to any more meetings with Mustafa after that last one, and Mustafa hadn't offered to take him to any more either. He felt frustrated because at the time he thought he had found something that was important; something where he could contribute and be respected. Now he wasn't so sure. Things hadn't gone exactly as he had thought they would at the meeting. The few who had been invited were friendly enough, but the tone had changed. Matt had tried to ask questions, but instead Abdullah started talking about infidels and the need to exterminate them. Who were the infidels? People who didn't believe in Islam? Like his parents? That didn't make sense to Matt. He thought everyone had the freedom of choice. Mustafa had wanted him to announce his acceptance of Islam at the meeting. But after listening to what Abdullah was saying, he couldn't. It didn't feel right. Maybe he was just a *chupa-medias*.

"It will be dark soon."

Matt turned around and saw Capt'n Mark. Matt was used to seeing Capt'n Mark wandering through the fields at dusk, checking on what had been accomplished that day. But he was surprised that Capt'n Mark had stopped to speak to him. He had been so intent on finishing the row, he hadn't even heard Capt'n Mark come up behind him.

"Yes, sir," said Matt, straightening up and involuntarily rubbing his lower back. Matt glanced around for his dad, but he was already back at the bus making sure none of the workers got left behind.

"You're a good worker, Matt," said Capt'n Mark. "You're smart and dependable, and you do a thorough job."

"Thank you, sir," said Matt. His bill hung limp against his leg. Capt'n Mark took the bill from Matt's hand and whacked a stalk of cane. The cut was clean, and the stalk fell in line with the other cane Matt had already cut.

"Have you ever thought about doing anything else?" asked Capt'n Mark. He whacked another stalk of cane.

Matt felt embarrassed. He had never told anyone about his dreams before. In fact, no one had ever asked.

"I'd like to be a cut foreman one day," he said standing a little straighter, "after I've learned more about the sugarcane business." He hoped the words didn't sound stupid, saying them out loud like that.

"That's a good goal to strive for," said Capt'n Mark, cutting three more stalks of cane. "Of course, there's a lot more to it than just knowing how to cut cane." He looked across the field of stubble freshly cut that day. "There are payrolls to keep up with, and work assignments, knowing how to get along with all kinds of people. And, of course, weekly reports have to be filled out—government forms, tax forms, insurance, that kind of thing. Things you would learn in school."

Capt'n Mark moved on down the row, cutting and stacking the stalks of cane as he did. Matt followed behind.

"The high school offers a course at night for people who work during the day. Some of the people who take it are your age. Others are older. Once they finish the course, they're given a high school diploma."

When Capt'n Mark finished the row, he handed the bill back to Matt.

"I'm thinking about expanding my sugarcane business. In another two or three years I want to clear that acreage that borders on the north pasture and plant it in cane. That would mean about five thousand more acres of sugarcane, and I would need another cut foreman to look after it for me."

It was almost totally dark now, but Matt could feel Capt'n Mark's eyes examining his face.

"Well, I guess that's all we can do here for today," Capt'n Mark said. He patted Matt on the back. "Think about it, Matt." And he turned and cut across the field toward the stables.

Matt followed the row of cut cane to the opposite end of the field where his dad was waiting to take him home.

"Everything all right?" his dad asked.

"Yeah," said Matt smiling. "I'm thinking about going to night school to earn my high school diploma."

Dan didn't say anything. He had worried about his son, dropping out of school the way he did. He had tried to talk to Matt about it at the time, about how it was a mistake not to get an education. But Matt's mind was made up and he wouldn't listen. He needed to hear it from someone else. Apparently, Matt had heard it from Jed Markham. Matt and his dad climbed into the pickup truck and headed for home.

AUGUST

Chapter Eleven

It was one of those bright, beautiful days when the sky was a brilliant cobalt blue contrasted only by an occasional white tuft of cloud. Dan and Evelyn Turpning, along with Jed Markham and Aunt Joyce, took their seats in what was called the guest box—those special seats reserved for the owners and guests of the entrants in the Gold Cup Equestrian Competition. Evelyn nervously smoothed a wrinkle on the sleeve of her new blouse, bought especially for this occasion to wear with her best summer slacks.

Capt'n Mark leaned forward as he watched several of the riders finish taking their horses through their final practice jumps. "The competition is stiff this year," he said to his two special guests. Dan reached for his wife's hand and held it. "The horses and the riders come from all over the world," he explained.

"Tillie is better than any of them," said Aunt Joyce. She sounded more confident than she felt. All of the riders Tillie would be competing against looked so much bigger—and older.

Matt wandered leisurely through the crowd checking out the people, the food booths, the concession stands, and, generally, anything else he happened upon. He would be able to watch Tillie and Arabesque from the bleachers next to the stadium and at the same time keep an eye on Mabe as his mom had asked him to do.

Mabe sat on her faded blue spread in a patch of shade under a group of palm trees within sight of the guest box, sketching in her pad with a charcoal pencil the horse trailers parked in the designated area nearby. Her green and purple basket was next to her.

Melissa watched from a fenced grassy area on the other side of the stadium field with Molly and Markette. They had the best view of the stadium from where they stood, and being away from the rest of the people and horses, Tillie and Arabesque would be able to spot them more easily.

Markette, sensing the excitement of the occasion, leaped into the air and then ran in a circle through the tall green grass a short distance away. When he realized that his mother wasn't with him, he ripped back to Molly's side, tail flying high, filled with the joyful exuberance of having experienced a brief moment of independence.

Arabesque knew the day was special. Earlier that morning the man who smelled like leather, tobacco, and wild cherries had clipped the "cat whiskers" from Arabesque's head and ears and had carefully washed and brushed her. Then he pulled her mane and tail into thick beautiful braids. Now Arabesque stood patiently with the small girl mounted on her back. Arabesque liked the small girl. Something about her airs—the smell of warm oats, sugar, and grass—reminded Arabesque of her best friend Molly and the foal. The small girl smelled friendly. As Arabesque watched each of the other horses perform and take their jumps, she quivered with excitement. She was eager for her turn.

Tillie, mounted on Arabesque, quietly waited apart from the other competitors. She was dressed in formal riding attire—black velvet helmet, white britches and white ratcatcher shirt, navy coat, and black field boots. On her hands were black leather gloves. Earlier, Melissa had fixed her hair in a French braid, and it hung down her back secured with a black silk ribbon.

She and Arabesque watched with interest as a big gray negotiated the stone wall, the vertical gate, the oxer, tiger trap, and the brush box. Six other riders had already completed the jumps. All six had knocked down barriers, therefore having points deducted from their final scores. One horse had simply refused to jump the water hazard and was disqualified. Now the big gray was going through the course, and so far it hadn't missed a single jump.

The spiderwort was coming up last. It was a complicated structure of vertical and horizontal rails and a fence, and it was the most difficult. Tillie and Arabesque watched as the big gray cleared it easily. Then the rider slapped the gray's neck with the end of the reins, urging it quickly to the finish line. But he was twelve seconds over the allowed time. That meant three points would be deducted from his score. And then Tillie heard the announcer:

> *Ladies and Gentlemen.*
> *Our final competitor for the National Gold Cup Equestrian Award, Youth Division, coming from Markham Farms, will be Arabesque. Riding Arabesque today is a newcomer to equestrian competition and also the youngest rider in today's event. May I introduce to you ...*
> *Miss Tillie Turpning!*

Tillie leaned forward and patted Arabesque on her neck. Then she whispered, "O.K., Arabesque. Let's show Molly what we can do."

The End

About the Author

Barbara Casey, originally from Carrollton, Illinois, attended the University of North Carolina, N.C. State University, and N.C. Wesleyan College where she received a BA degree, summa cum laude, with a double major in English and history. In 1978 she left her position as Director of Public Relations and Vice President of Development at North Carolina Wesleyan College to write full-time.

Ms. Casey has written over a dozen award-winning books of fiction and nonfiction for both young adults and adults. The awards include the National Association of University Women Literary Award, the Sir Walter Raleigh Literary Award, the Independent Publisher Book Award, the Dana Award for Outstanding Novel, the IP Best Book for Regional Fiction, among others.